Dog and Cat

Dog and Cat

Written by Paul Fehlner

Illustrated by Maxie Chambliss

children's press®

A Division of Scholastic Inc.

New York Toronto London Auckland Sydney
Mexico City New Delhi Hong Kong
Danbury, Connecticut

Library of Congress Cataloging-in-Publication Data

Fehlner, Paul.
  Dog and cat / written by Paul Fehlner ; illustrated by Maxie
Chambliss.– [1st American ed.].
      p. cm. – (My first reader)
Summary: Due to their physical limitations, an old dog and a fat cat
live together relatively peacefully.
  ISBN 0-516-22924-9 (lib. bdg.)   0-516-24626-7 (pbk.)
  [1. Dogs–Fiction. 2. Cats–Fiction. 3. Stories in rhyme.] I.
Chambliss, Maxie, ill. II. Title. III. Series.
  PZ8.3.F325Do 2003
  [E]–dc21
                              2003003611

3 4 5 6 7 8 9 10 R 12 11 10 09 08 07

Note to Parents and Teachers

Once a reader can recognize and identify the 20 words
used to tell this story, he or she will be able to read successfully
the entire book. These 20 words are repeated throughout the story,
so that young readers will be able to easily recognize
the words and understand their meaning.

The 20 words used in this book are:

cannot	good	quite
can't	he	run
chase	is	silly
cat	like	that
dog	not	the
fat	old	too
for	pair	

The dog is old.

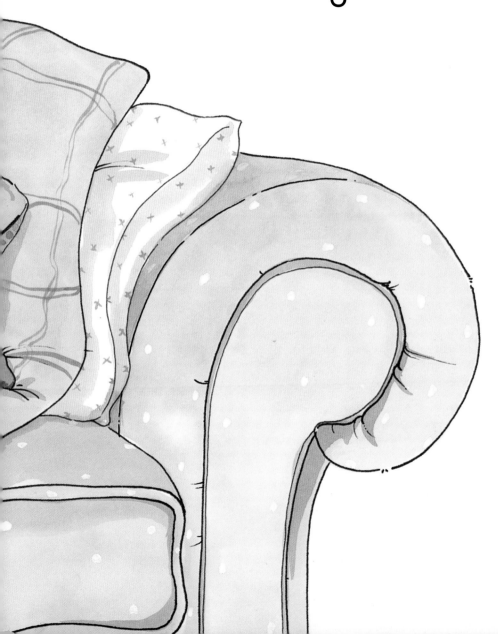

The cat is fat.

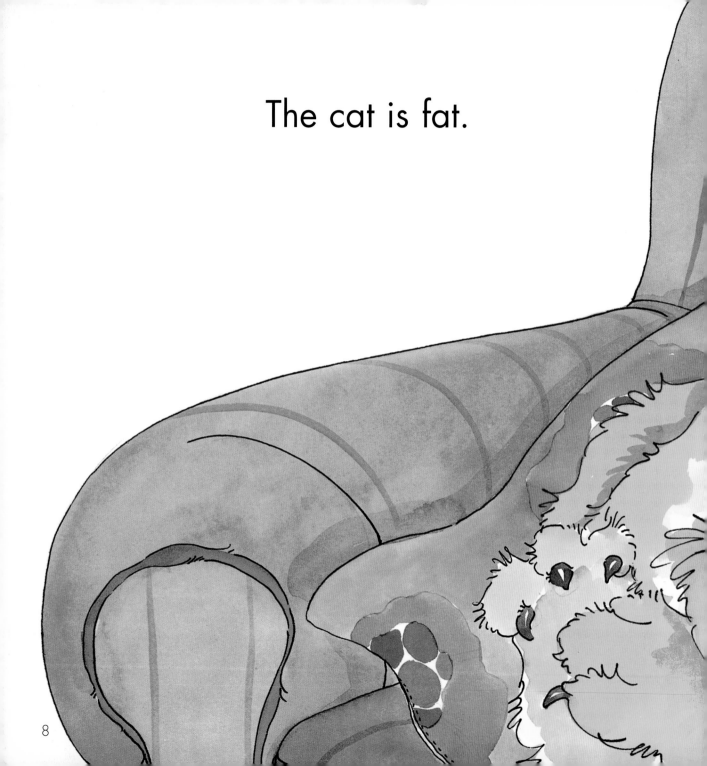

The old, old dog

can't chase the cat.

The dog is old,

not like the cat.

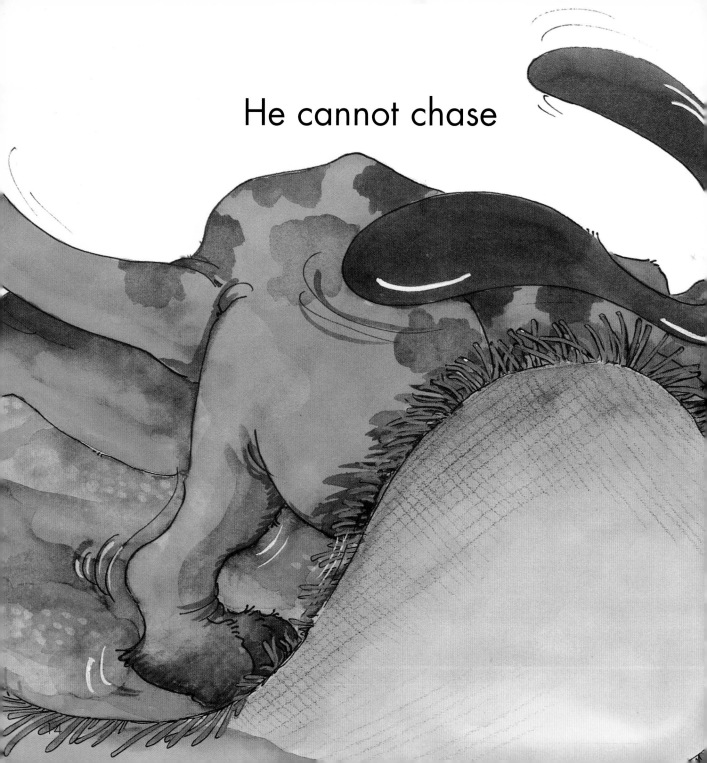

He cannot chase

the fat, fat cat.

That is quite good,

for the fat cat.

The cat can't run.

He is too fat.

That silly pair,

the dog, the cat.

The dog is old.

The cat is fat.

ABOUT THE AUTHOR

Paul Fehlner is an intellectual property attorney with five children and three dogs. He and his family live in New Jersey.

ABOUT THE ILLUSTRATOR

Maxie Chambliss is the illustrator of more than forty books for children. She lives with her family in Somerville, Massachusetts.